Exhibition

A Taboo Erotica Short Story

BY JULI VALENTI

Synopsis

Everyone has their kinks… ranging from the extreme to the subdued.

Haven is aware of hers and, after spending the last six years searching for the elusive, almost non-existent secret society, La Petite Mort, she finally found them.

Or, rather, they found her.

Desire. Secrets hidden within the soul.

Delve deeper down the rabbit hole and see just how far your own kinks may go.

Copyright © 2023 Juli Valenti

All rights reserved. No part of this publication may be reproduced, distributed, or transmitted in any form or by any means, including photocopying, recording, or other electronic or mechanical methods, without the prior written permission from the author, except in the case of brief quotations embodied in critical reviews and certain other noncommercial uses permitted by copyright law.

This book is a work of fiction. Names, characters, places and incidents are products of the author's imagination or are used fictitiously. Any resemblance to actual events, locales, or persons living or dead, is entirely coincidental.

First Edition. Printed in the United States of America.
ISBN: 9798861159395

Cover Created by Phycel Designs
www.Phycel.com

To all the girls with hidden kinks.

Le Petite Mort

Your presence is greatly desired and requested at the Masquerade.

Twenty-fourth day of September

Eight o'clock

Formal dress and masquerade attire required.

Transportation to be provided.

I stared at the invitation, caressing the heavy yardstick edges between two fingers. The nondescript envelope had been delivered to my office sometime through the morning, though I wasn't sure when or from whom. My name was elegantly scrawled across the front in impossibly beautiful gold script, but nothing else marred the fine paper. No return address, no post stamp, nothing. Merely my name and an enclosed with a gold wax seal. Even the event address was curiously missing from the missive.

The fact I'd received the invitation at all left me speechless. I'd studied *Le Petite Mort* for years, borderline obsessed with the elusive group. For all intents and purposes, they were the whispers behind closed doors, rumors among certain proper crowds. Think high-end sorority or fraternity, underground, with no invitation, no rush parties, or pledges. *Secret society* would be a better descriptive term, but I dismissed the thought as quickly as it came. *Le Petite Mort* was anything but cheesy, and that was how secret society made it sound.

Le Petite Mort wasn't a run of the mill group, full of spoiled rich kids jumping off buildings and yelling in Latin because they could. There were no fancy parties with avoided letters and words, nor gorilla face masks and ballgowns. No Greek letters adorned a fancy million-dollar mansion, girls didn't wear sweatshirts proudly detailing their abbreviations, and there were certainly no chapters throughout the county.

They were so much more than all of that.

You see, there are certain inalienable truths when it comes to human beings. In general, Homo sapiens are social creatures, requiring the presence of others to maintain sanity and peace of mind. Without socialization, all humans will fall into despair and crumple when left to their own solitude. Humans also desire pleasure, though the sort of things that drive this pleasure varies from person to person.

For some, pleasure is simply building a large family, complete with the white picket fence and Fido the golden retriever. Others crave the arts, from books and magazines. The arts are driven by those seeking visual or audible pleasure, encompassing the realms of dance, music, paintings, statues and architecture and the like. Some find pleasure in crafts, creating something from nothing in the comfort of their homes - ranging from making beautiful floral wreaths to crocheting penises and basking in the great differences of each one. I'm not one to judge, but I know the latter brings great joy to a few.

And then, there are people like me. People who crave pleasure, erotic and undeniable pleasure. This pleasure, is a carnal pleasure, one that drives the soul and every instinct a human being possesses. It is the kiss in a dark alley from a handsome stranger, a gentle caress on that smooth skin below the breasts, and the unexpected moan escaping your lips. It is creativity in the bedroom, complete with a laundry list of toys, or secret quickies before a board meeting.

Me? Yeah, I have my own kinks, the secrets locked deep within my gut.

They are, after all, what attracted me to *La Petite Mort* to begin with.

Growing up, I was a pretty average girl. I was the youngest child in a family of four, with two parents working an average nine to five job, and an average relationship with an older brother who relentlessly picked on me. I was never popular nor unpopular, rather keeping to myself and my own crew of average friends. I sang in choir, did well enough in school to get a scholarship, and went off to an average college. I wasn't prom queen, nor valedictorian, not rich nor poor. Perfectly average.

Once I hit college, however, is when my life as I knew it would change. I'd never lived away from my family, or somewhere that cohabitation and mingling was so easily acceptable. There were very few rules in college, so I did what any sheltered, average girl would do - I rushed a sorority. I wore the sweatshirt and had a big sister to show me the ropes; I got hazed like all the rest and went cow-tipping in stiletto heels. And I met boys… a lot of them.

Some of the frat guys were vanilla if vanilla tasted like boredom by sex. Drunk and grunting cavemen, eager to have their rods touched and egos stroked. But Christian? He was the one who really awoke something in me, the exotic flavors that life had to offer.

Christian was handsome-ish, in a dark, why did you join a fraternity kind of way. He was… different. He read poetry and listened to classical music. He laughed when jokes were funny and had a penchant for watching old sitcoms to pick up on nuances that were written into the script and missed. Regardless of what was going on around him, Christian remained laser focused on anything that interested him… including me. He would be the last and final Sigma Alpha I was ever involved in, the one who haunted me in between my sheets and whose memory still caresses the deepest, darkest parts of my soul. No other has ever measured up to him, not then and not now.

It was with Christian I learned the great pleasures that could be found in the touch of a man. The location in which that passion and pleasure was found never mattered for Christian, either: when his dick got hard, all bets were off. Fucking on the law of the frat house, in the living room during the many frat parties, even in the stacks of the library surrounded by *ahem* eager freshman.

Thus, my kinks were born, blossomed, watered, and encouraged.

For me, I like to watch sex; more, I enjoy *being* watched.

I enjoy feeling not only the desire of my partner as their hands roam my body, but the desire of those around me, too. It just does something for me.

Now, I'm not saying I want to be railed in the middle of Time Square during rush hour... mostly. I'm not harboring some great calling of being a pornstar in the middle of some dirty warehouse gang bang for the entire world to see. I guess it's complicated to explain.

So how does *La Petite Mort* come into play?

It was one night, the last night... the final time Christian and I were together - atop the common building in the middle of the quad, above the great campus' clock.

The bright lights shone against Christian's skin, shimmering amongst the fine sheen of sweat that covered the sinews of his body. I was Icarus flying too close to the sun, blinded by the promise in the man before me, and I didn't care that we could get caught. There was always that risk, as our sexcapades had become more and more scandalous and daring. But, as always, it didn't matter to me, so long as the man touched me. Luckily, he didn't care any more than I did.

His hands reached for me, pulling me into the beaming light that shone on the bell tower, creating a spotlight just for us. He pressed my naked breasts against his chest, my nipples grazing his skin and raising goosebumps across my flesh.

"You're so fucking beautiful like this. The whole world should see the beauty in your body, in your sex, in your passion."

His words were a growl and I melted against him. I moaned and his hand snaked between us, his fingers grazing my wetness. My body eagerly begged for his touch, just as it always did.

"So fucking beautiful," he murmured, pulling away and sucking my juices from his fingers. My body shivered, though from the action or from the lack of his body heat, I wasn't sure.

Gently, he stepped forward, his heat warming me instantly, and his lips captured mine. The kiss started softly, hesitantly, playfully before turning heated, his tongue meeting mine and entwining. My leg wrapped around his hip and his hand gripped first my thigh, before moving to my ass, pulling my sex against his. He was hard, ready, and I involuntarily gasped into his mouth. A small smile curved his lips as he pulled back, knowing I would do just about anything to feel him inside me.

He tipped his head to the side, his eyes hooded and full of sensuality. It was a question, unasked, and I nodded. At that he grinned and turned me to face the quad and courtyard below. I briefly noted that there were student straggling around, the sun having only just set. Final evening classes had yet to adjourn, and people milled about - whether they were aware of what was going above them, I didn't know, but I liked to think they did.

Christian's body grazed my back and I shuddered, knowing what was coming. He guided my arms down to grip the concrete barrier, effectively bending me over and giving him a perfect view of the deepest parts of me. His groan was my reward, followed by his hand once again trailing up my thighs and finding my wetness. He toyed with me, his fingers entering me only to pull away and play with my clit. It was delicious but I wanted his cock. I whined, peering back at him with wanting eyes and a chuckle escaped him.

He nodded, pressing the head of his cock between my fold, hesitating for only the slightest of seconds. A mere moment in time, as he took in the passerby below, those surrounding us. And, with that, he thrust into me, hard, drawing a shriek of pleasure from my throat. It took my pussy a heartbeat to adjust to his hardness, his length - the man was not a 'small' man. The head of his dick pressed against my cervix, something many may find painful, but I relished in. I loved it. I wanted it. I wanted him.

Pulling back, he thrust again, and again, his balls slapping loudly against my folds and my ass. Christian's rhythm was punishing, unyielding, and delectable, all at once, as he filled me. His hand occasionally came down on the tender skin of my ass, the sound echoing against the building and into the night. I needed all he had to offer, each slap, each thrust. I wanted everything he had to offer in those moments. None of it would ever be enough.

Without missing a beat, Christian snaked his arm around me, his fingers delving between my folds.

Before I could process, his fingers were pressing on my clit and I moaned, loudly. I couldn't help my body's reaction as it shuddered, overwhelmed by the onslaught of sensations coursing through me. He knew the exact pressure, the exact flick of his fingertips that would drive me wild as he continued to pound into me from behind. He was relentless and it only took mere moments more for my body to quiver, my fingers painfully pressing into the concrete I held on to.

"Cum for me."

His words were a command, authoritative, with no room to do little else than what he demanded. And, just as he'd trained it to, my body obeyed. I screamed, my body skyrocketing through its orgasm; I left my body and met the stars, naming them as my soul floated into space, and the world below spun. Christian stilled as his body, too, found release. His fingers at my hip dug into my skin, an unrelenting hold to keep himself upright, leaving what I knew would be bruises later.

We remained connected, our breathing a matching rhythm for what seemed like forever. But, as his cock went limp and fell away from my body, so did he. I sighed, sadly, at the loss of his warmth as he moved back and I turned, taking small solace in our mutual pleasure running down my leg.

"I think all of campus got to hear you that time," Christian said, pride tinging his tone, his large, movie-star smile spanning his face and alighting his eyes. But, there was something else in his expression, a sorrow that neither of us could erase.

"Do you really have to leave?" I asked, not for the first time and hating how pathetic I sounded. With the lack of his body heat the crispness in the newly-spring air was uncomfortable across my skin and I folded my arms around my breasts. I didn't want to be as exposed as I was; I hadn't cared who'd witness our sex, but this vulnerability? No, this I didn't want anyone to see. Not even Christian.

He remained silent for what seemed like forever, his eyes taking in our surroundings before locking in on my face. I started to move toward my clothes, fearing he wouldn't answer at all, before he spoke.

"You know I have to, Haven. I have no choice. This is as much a part of life as our sex."

"But, you could stay —"

"Haven," he paused, swallowing hard and running a hand over his face. "I graduated last

semester. I stayed this semester because I can't get enough of you. My father is waiting for me."

I knew it was true. His father, the CEO of some big, hot shot bank, had been blowing Christian's phone up for weeks, demanding to know when he was finally going to get his shit together and go to work like he was supposed to. I felt guilty, and grateful, that he'd stayed, but the weight of his father's threats had become too much for either of us to bear.

"I would stay with you, if I could. You still have another years here, and then you're off to law school. This is what has to happen," Christian said softly, moving toward me and using his finger to tip my chin up, my eyes meeting his. "This isn't goodbye. Not for you, nor for me. This isn't the end of the sex you enjoy, either. Find La Petite Mort - that's where I'll be waiting for you."

"La -"

"Get your things, Haven. It's getting late and as loud as you were, I'm surprised we didn't set off the bell," Christian interrupted, silencing me. "I'll walk you back to the house."

That had been the last evening I'd spent with Christian, the last time I'd found someone who so completely met every sexual kink I never knew I had. It was also the last public display of desire I'd gotten to take part of - men these days just don't seem to have a sense of adventure. Unless, of course, they're drug addicts or alcoholics, looking for a good time. Neither option was really my cup of tea.

Six years was a long time, an eternity when my life wasn't that long to begin with. Six years of mediocre sex and daydreams. That thought was depressing in and of itself.

"Haven!" a high-pitched voice called from over my shoulder, shaking me from my revelry. "Whatcha got there?"

I quickly moved papers to cover the invitation, hoping if I played stupid that Tiffany wouldn't notice. It had worked more than once, so it wasn't a long shot.

"Oh nothing. Just going through the latest briefings from the Sadie case," I answered, picking up a highlighter. "Did you get the interrogatories from West?"

Tiffany arched an eyebrow before opening her mouth to speak. Whatever she had been about to say, she changed her mind and instead nodded. "Earlier today. I'll get them for you."

I nodded, waving a hand and turning back to my computer screen. I forced my mind to focus on the somber case of Sadie, whose only regular dance partner was that of her drugs.

"What the hell am I supposed to wear?" I yelled to my closet, hoping something would jump out at me. It had been a week since I'd received my invitation to *Le Petit Mort* and it was officially the twenty fourth of September. Since its arrival, the gold elegant script had haunted me, flooding me with memories of Christian, and excitement. Though none of those emotions helped me to choose a formal dress for the event.

What did one wear to a pseudo secret society that was named after an orgasm?

I had no idea what to expect; no idea if this was going to be a fancy tea and crumpets event or if I'd be laden with fancy food and a silent auction. No one knew who the members of the group were, so I wasn't going to know anyone once I got there, unless *he* was there. Though, because it was a masquerade, my chances of finding him were that of a needle in a haystack.

What was formal attire? A ball gown? A little black dress? Formal meant a lot of different things depending on who you were, too. I didn't want to get it wrong and the options that had coursed through my head drove me insane for days. I'd gone to multiple stores, bought several different dresses, though I couldn't make a decision.

"It really shouldn't be this hard, Haven. Pick a stupid fucking dress. You've been waiting for this, searching for this, and you're going to bitch and moan about wearing something formal? You're a lawyer for goddamn sake, you can come up with something and argue the pros and cons later."

I'd told no one at the office about the invitation, though I'd requested the day before the event and the week after it off. I probably didn't need to do so, but I wanted time to decompress, from whatever awaited me. If the whole thing was a stupid sham that I'd spent years chasing all because some stupid frat boy had mentioned it while I was naked, I was going to be pissed. And, if it wasn't, I was going to need some time. I never missed work, so no one batted an eye.

I spent the previous day doing all the womanly things I tended to let fall by the wayside. I got a manicure and a pedicure, my hair touched up and trimmed, and my eyebrows micro-something'ed. Earlier I'd put my hair up in curlers, piling it daintily atop my head. All I had left was to pick a dress.

The clock on the bedside flashed seven o'clock. I was out of time - whoever my transportation was would more than likely be there at any time. Frustrated, I grabbed the empire formal gown I'd purchased the day before and slipped into it. It zipped easily up the back and flattered my curves. I stepped in front of the full-length mirror to take in my reflection, grateful my makeup remained perfect and that my stress hadn't messed anything. I slipped my stockinged feet into my black pumps and nodded to my reflection. This was as good as average me was going to get.

Sighing, I made my way to the kitchen, pulling a mini-Fireball from the freezer. I needed to take the edge off my nerves and my old faithful, favorite cinnamon drink was just what the doctor ordered. It was blessedly cold, the warmth a welcome burn as I drank the contents of the small bottle. I debated a second one as my toe tapped anxiously against the tile floor. But I thought better of it and instead slipped one into the small clutch purse I'd wrapped around my wrist. I needed to stay level, prepared, for whatever may be awaiting me.

"Plus, if you're getting kidnapped and killed, at least you'll have Fireball for the ride," I said to the air around me, checking my watch for the umpteenth time. This waiting thing really wasn't my jam, but I didn't know what I was supposed to do, or if I was supposed to go downstairs and wait in front of the building. This was all new to me, and the invitation only stated that transportation would be provided…

it hadn't said from where, or what time exactly. The unknowing was making me jittery.

Right on cue, a knock sounded at the door, startling me. I took a deep breath before moving toward it. For a heartbeat, I debated *not* answering, not opening it. I hadn't signed up for anything - I could absolutely pretend I wasn't home. Hell, I could totally crawl into bed, pull the covers up, and pretend I'd never even been invited. No one would know, really, except me… and whoever found me to invite me anyway.

What if the whole invitation was a trick? What if some dark web hackers had come across my many online searches and decided to play practical jokes? Worse, what if there were no jokes? What if I really *was* setting myself up for my own kidnapping and subsequent, gruesome murder? Anything was possible - I watched programs all the time on crime tv, often yelling at the woman of the horrific storyline. The ones where you yell "don't go in there!" even though you know they're going to and that they will die in some unimaginable, awful way. I liked to think I was smarter than that. Whether I was… was clearly a different story.

I released a breath I hadn't realized I'd been holding and shook my head. For years I'd played the role of Alice, delving deeper down the rabbit hole. I'd been searching for so long. *La Petite Mort* was within my grasp, having quite literally fallen onto my desk, and there was no way in Hell I was going to pass up the opportunity to explore the lucrative group. If the night ended up being a giant farce, at least I would know I tried. At least I knew I'd exhausted all avenues, all search engines, all connections, to find my holy grail.

Opening the door, I found myself face to face with a tall, dark-skinned man, dressed to the nines. His tux was neatly pressed, his tie done in a precise Windsor knot, and his shoes polished to a mirror shine. He held a black chauffeur hat, tucked neatly under his left arm. As he saw me, he smiled, reaching his face, revealing slight lines around his eyes. His expression held a kindness that soothed at least a percentage of my nerves. A tiny percentage, that, but something was better than nothing.

"Car service, Miss," he said, his words a deep southern drawl. He dipped his head as he said it, in a slight bow, that I wasn't sure what to do with. "Lawrence," he added, nodding again. "Please."

I was confused for just a moment, the 'please' throwing me, until I realized he was holding out an arm in offering gesture. I nodded and pulled the door shut behind me, pressing numbers into the keypad to lock it. I appreciated he had the grace to keep his eyes averted as I entered the code, though something told me if he really wanted inside anywhere, let alone my apartment, a lock probably wouldn't stop him.

Accepting his proffered arm, I allowed him to lead me to the elevator, holding my breath as we stepped inside and it began its descent. I hated small spaces to begin with, but being in small places with strangers, going to strange places, made it even worse.

"I'm Haven," I introduced myself awkwardly. I only just stopped myself from rattling off random details about who I was as a person, too. I'd read somewhere that the more information you gave people would help you in a survival situation - if they saw you as a person, a life, they were less likely to kill you.

"I know, Miss," he answered, not an ounce of sarcasm present in his tone. But still, his words made me feel stupid.

Of course he knows who you are, stupid. He was sent to your home *to pick you up.*

Either *La Petite Mort* had their hands in more things than I thought was possible, or, it really was a murder set up.

Too late now.

As the elevator doors opened, my heart rate beating a techno beat, I allowed Lawrence to escort me through the building lobby. I nodded to Charlie, the old man who manned the door, as he continued our path out the main entrance and up to a tinted black town car. It was just shy of being a limo, without the pomp and circumstances, though I couldn't tell if that made me happy or slightly disappointed. I wasn't getting murdered in a limo, so that would mean it would be a much more compact crime scene for sure.

He opened the back door for me and extended a hand to help me lower myself into the lush leather seat. There was a golden box set to the side, with a matching gold ribbon holding it closed. I glanced up at my chauffeur, and he read my unasked question.

"For you," he affirmed, though having settled myself I could see the tag, my name scrawled in the same fancy script that had adorned the invitation itself. I nodded to Lawrence so he knew I'd heard him and, after he ensured my dress was in the car, he shut the door.

I picked up the fancy box, the lightness of it surprising; something enclosed in gold should always feel a hefty weight, but this was feather light. I desperately wanted to know what was in it, to open it like a five-year-old on Christmas morning with full permission from their parents. But, on the other hand, I also really wanted to watch where we were driving to, make mental notes of the landmarks around us. Of course, the window tinting was dark, which made it tougher to see out of, but it was still doable. Torn, I worried the ribbon between my fingers, looking between the gift box and the window as Lawrence pulled away from the curb and began our journey to the unknown.

Eventually curiosity overtook my rationale, or irrationale, depending on who was debating my actions. I gingerly pulled one end of the ribbon, and the other, allowing the bow to fall away from the ornate package. Picking the lid off the box, I peered inside to find golden tissue paper, and something black. I lifted it out of its wrapping and turned it from side to side.

It was a masquerade mask, beautifully made with black silk and lace. Occasional rhinestones sprinkled around the eyes, creating an elegance and intrigue along the fabric. It was stunning, and just as light as the package had portrayed it, with matching silk ribbon extending from both sides to attach it. I was surprised it was more than just a lacy face mask, the kind girls buy on Amazon for costume parties; it was stunning in its intricacy, with a fancy feather plume accented the right side, attached with a single emerald green gem. It was delicate and would cover almost the entirety of my face.

Good thing I didn't spend too much time on my makeup, I thought wryly. The mask was going to do exactly what it was supposed to do - completely hide who I was. The only thing that would be seen through it were my red lips and my eyes, and *those* were done with the precision I lacked in all my other makeup. Somewhere along the way in life I'd mastered the art of eyeliner, mascara, and eye shadow… my only makeup strength.

Something glinted in the box and I double checked, worried I may have missed something. There, was a lightweight mirror. *La Petite Mort* had thought of everything. Dutifully, I withdrew the mirror and propped it awkwardly in my lap as I placed the mask against my face, the silk a cool caress against my skin. It was impossible to explain, but the moment it was expertly tied and anchored, with the use of a couple of the safety pins I'd used to style my hair, I felt better. It was as if it was a safety net, an allowance to leave Haven behind, and be someone else entirely. I guess that is the point of masks to begin with.

All too quickly, the car came to a stop, and Lawrence opened his door. I was surprised - it didn't seem like we'd traveled that long. A quick glance at my watch told me we'd only been driving for twenty minutes or so… so wherever we were going had been under my nose the entire time.

With the same flourish he'd opened my door outside my building, he repeated opening my door once again and offering me a hand. I took it, allowing him to steady me on my heels and smoothing my dress as I looked around me. We were in front of a large, three-story white marble building, the pillars shining in the sunset. A good twenty steps lead to the entryway in a matching marble, no railing marring the perfect surface of the precious carved stones.

To my surprise, Lawrence didn't get back in the car and leave me at the steps. Instead, he gently tucked my hand in the crook of his arm once more, softly patting the back of my hand. He smiled to himself as he escorted me up each step, matching his much larger pace to mine, before reaching the doorway. A deep scarlet carpet had been placed in front of the ornate closed doors, but no one opened them for us. I glanced up at the larger man and he patted my hand once more.

"This is as far as I go. You must enter of your own desire… for desire does not come to those who do not reach for it."

With that, he dipped his head once more, and, leaving me alone in front of a giant, foreign building, made his way back to the car. I watched as he climbed back into the town car, his fingers touching the brim of his hat before shutting the door. I watched as he started the engine, the sound a whisper in the wind, and I watched as he drove away.

At least you're not going to be murdered, not in a limo.

I peered up at the ornate doors, the gold filagree decorating the jam around it. The handles were old and just as detailed as the doors themselves, old, gold, and decorated with old fashioned-lion heads. I took a deep breath, hoping for the best, and grasped one and pulled, allowing the cold air to sooth the humid Texas air.

Here we go.

Wherever I was, I most certainly was no longer in Kansas, Toto.

The inside of the giant building was breathtaking, stunning, probably the most elegant building I'd ever seen in my entire life. It was something that ancient writers spoke of, that artists painted, and people with a great deal of money longed to recreate.

Decorated in the same scarlet color of the carpet, what looked like velvet or suede chaise lounges lined the entry way, red tapestries expertly hanging from the ceiling. The starkest difference was the color; how the outside was white marble, the inside marble was black. A deep, striated black, with flecks of gold and silvers swirling to mix. The contrast between the red and black was just something that didn't exist in a normal world.

Unsure of myself, and trying to take in everything around me, I forced my feet to move forward. Walking deeper through the main hall, I prayed for some sign of life, though I didn't see anyone else.

And here you are, walking around in a formal gown with a mask on your face. You probably look stupid, Haven. What have you gotten yourself into?

I ignored my internal skeptic. I knew she had a point, but it didn't feel that way. It felt like so much more… like I'd walked into a different world, which was what I'd been hoping for. The carpet seemed to be a guide and I followed it, sighing in relief as I came to a marble countertop, with two gold mask clad women behind it. They wore identical, simple black dresses, that were neatly tailored to fit but not anything like the gown I'd donned. I suddenly felt incredibly overdressed.

"Hello," the one on the right, the blonde, greeted.

"Your name?" Asked the other, the brunette on the left.

Their voices were the same, a melodic soprano that echoed against the marble around us. There was little inflection in the short words, nothing to indicate whether they were kind or not.

"Um," I faltered, unsure if I was to give my entire given name, or just my first name. "Haven," I answered, before thinking better of it and adding, "Haven Silverlain."

"Welcome, Haven," the blonde said, her voice the same singsong melody.

"We hope you find the desires you hide from the rest of the world inside," the other replied, her voice a perfect harmony to the blonde. "But first, you must check your things. Do not fret, as nothing will be removed and will be returned to you once the night has come to its completion."

I nodded in understanding. It made complete sense. I unwrapped the rhinestone wrist strap for my clutch and handed it over to the brunette. She nodded and peered up at me expectantly. After a moment, I shifted nervously, looking from my purse to the masked girls.

"That's the only thing I brought," I told them dumbly. It was Texas, too hot for a jacket ninety-nine percent of the time, and there were no pockets in my dress. Idly I realized that my Fireball was tucked in the clutch they were checking for me. *Damn.*

"I apologize," the blonde said, her voice reflecting the most emotion I'd heard in her since having arrived. She moved from around the marble countertop and made her way to my side. "We were not aware that this is your first time."

"It is."

"Desire doesn't come to those who do not reach for it," the brunette said, with the same kindness the blonde had adopted. It took me a moment to realize she was echoing the same words Lawrence had said before leaving me in front of the doors.

"If you are to reach that which you seek, you must enter with an open mind. Here, there are no judgements. The only boundaries inside are the boundaries which we place on ourselves, rather than those we wrap around ourselves to hide from the world."

"Do you understand?"

I shook my head. I didn't understand. I mean, I understand the words in which they were spoken, just not necessarily in the context they were meant.

The blonde smiled gently. "You must check not only your clutch, but also your gown. We enter the doors ahead without the coverings that hide our desires."

"If you'll turn, I can help."

She doesn't mean.

She couldn't mean.

Judging by the expectant expressions on gold one and gold two, they most certainly did. They were instructing me to disrobe, to go inside in my underwear. Was I wearing underwear? I wasn't wearing a bra, as I didn't need one with the gown I'd chosen. I did a mental inventory of what all I was wearing. Mask. Gown. Stiletto heels. Thigh-high fishnet stockings. Yep, felt like I was wearing underwear, so that was a plus. No bra.

"Um," I muttered, nervously, still undecided on if this was something I could or wanted to do. Did I have the self-confidence to enter a room full of strangers, wearing nothing but what remained under my dress? Was I allowed to keep my shoes?

"Of course you may keep your shoes - they are delicious," the brunette told me, making me realize I must've asked the last question aloud.

Okay…

I could leave. I could still leave, turn, and run, and never assuage my search for *La Petite Mort*. Maybe if I yelled loudly, Lawrence would come back from where he'd disappeared to, and would take me home.

Or, I could go with it. Hell, I fantasized about fucking in public. To relive the days I'd been able to and would've given anything to repeat. Of course, back then my body was a bit tighter than it was now… but I was still in good shape. I still went to the gym a couple times a week.

Nodding, I turned my back to Gold Two who'd offered to help. With cold, small hands, she grasped the zipper and released it. With great care she and Gold One helped me step out of the dress, ensuring I was steady on my feet before she moved through a doorway and out of my sight. I hadn't realized a doorway there had existed, and I was assuming she was hanging the dress up.

I stood awkwardly, unsure what to do with my hands. Instinct told me to raise them to cover my now exposed breasts - the cold air which had felt good and refreshing when I'd arrived now causing my nipples to pucker to tight buds. But I fought the urges of my instincts. I couldn't walk around with my arms crossed the entire night, and, as of right now, it was only Gold One and I in the hallway.

This was definitely a first. If someone had told me an hour ago I'd be in some great marble building, mostly naked, I would've laughed at them. Or maybe I wouldn't have… but it would've been nice to have had *some* warning. At least my purple panties weren't granny panties, and I had shaved my legs. And I knew for a fact my legs looked great in my stilettos - the fishnet thigh highs just a nice decoration.

Chalk this shit up to things I never would've guessed.

This hadn't played a part in any of my true crime scenarios. Of course, it was a way better alternative than my overactive imagination, but still.

"Nothing you do not wish to happen will happen, Haven," Gold One spoke, retreated to her previous post behind the countertop. "We respect boundaries for those who have them; however, this is not the place for games. Participate if you choose, or don't - that decision is yours and yours alone. But remember, there is no judgement. We all think differently, as desire flourishes differently for everyone inside."

"I understand," I told her, this time fully meaning it. I knew my kinks. I knew everyone else had different ones. As I said before… crochet penises. I don't judge.

Gold One smiled broadly, waving her hand in presentation of the doors just beyond the counter. "Go on. Welcome to *La Petite Mort*, Haven."

Opening the doors beyond the Golden Girls' perch, I was filled with emotions I could barely comprehend myself. I was excited, moisture pooling between my legs an indicator it was both personally and sexually. I was nervous. I was intimidated. And I was terrified.

Forcing my heeled feet forward, I entered the room, this time assaulted by bodies, music, and colors. Dozens of people lined the large room, this one bigger than even the entry way. It was impossibly large, the size of two or three normal ballrooms, all decorated in the same scarlet red draping. Various furniture of the same color and fabric was placed throughout the room, from what I could see through the sea of people. But this, was certainly not high tea or a silent auction.

To my right, a couple were locked in an embrace, their bodies pressed tightly together. She wore no panties and even at my angle I could tell his fingers were buried inside her. Her hips gyrated softly against his hand, as another female body came up behind the man, running her hands up his thighs and around gripping his ass. I wanted to keep watching. I wanted to look away. I wanted to do anything other than stay frozen, entranced by the scene.

And so I moved, deeper into the room. Couples, trios, and more were everywhere, everyone in the same state of dress, or less, than I was. Some were naked, some were clothes in straps that covered nothing, though were for sexual pleasure. I no longer felt under dressed or over dressed and I was actually grateful that Gold One and Gold Two had taken my gown away. There was no way I could've gone into this room … dressed.

Waiters flitted around the room, carrying small trays of drinks and I snagged one of the champagne flutes as one passed by, nodding my thanks. His eyes trailed my body, taking in my flesh and he smiled softly before moving onward.

I continued through the sea of scarlet, of moans and sucking sounds, weighing the way in which I felt about it. It wasn't what I'd anticipated, but it wasn't shocking or surprising. I wasn't shocked or scandalized by the views around me. If anything, I was intrigued. That inner part of me I tried so often to hide all but stretched in anticipation inside me. My kinks liked being around others who didn't try to cover up their desires. It was… all consuming.

Hypnotic music filtered through the air, though the source was lost to me. The rhythms were intoxicating, the kind you wanted to move, and be moved, to. All around me were people intertwined and I took a moment to take in the view once more. I gravitated toward a couple, the woman bent over a chaise lounge, the man behind her. His tanned skin shone with sweat, despite the chill of the air conditioning, and he alternated between caressing the bare, milky skin of her ass and using a whip to punish her. She moaned at both touches, her head thrown back and her hair tumbling to fall across her back.

My gaze found another woman, her body laying prone across the floor. Several others circled her, their mouths meeting her skin and hands pouring some sort of liquid across her. Lips met lips, hands trailing over the other. It was erotic and sensual and nothing I'd ever seen. And, if any of the participants were bothered by my voyeurism, none made it noticeable. It was more than they were so enthralled, so captured by those around them, that no one else existed.

Turning, I realized I was in the center of the great room, my attention having been captured by the many shows around me. There, in the middle, was a scarlet chaise lounge, curiously empty. My feet hurt and I desperately wanted to sit for a moment, take a second to breathe through the thick sexuality that filled the air. But, I also wasn't sure the rules. The Golden Girls had told me that nothing I didn't want to happen would be forced on me, but what if sitting down was an invitation? Did I want to *not* invite someone to me? I wasn't sure of the answer, torn in my desires, leaving me decision less and standing despite the pain from my fierce shoes.

A large body brushed against me and I spun. I expected the owner of the rigid muscles before me to back away but they didn't, and my nipples grazed his hard chest. A gasp of pleasure escaped my lips before I could stop it.

"Haven."

My name was a reverent whisper, a word so barely spoken I was almost certain I'd missed it. It was a voice I'd long dreamed about, had known for many years only to have had it swept away the same way it'd appeared. It was the voice I fantasized about, and that I'd longed to hear once more.

"Christian?"

I'd meant my reply to be a certainty the same as mine had been from him, but it wasn't. It came out as a question, a disbelief in the sea of bodies around us. The music still pumped around us, and I questioned if I'd had more to drink than I realized, though I don't think that was it. It was more I was falling under a spell I didn't want to break.

"My Haven," he murmured, his head bending for his lips to take mine, and I let him. The moment his mouth met mine, I knew I'd made the right decision. I knew that if this was the last day, if it had all been fake and a ruse, this would've made it worth it.

His tongue snaked out to find mine, tasting of champagne and sweetness and Christian. I returned the gesture with the same fervor, pressing my breasts tighter to his body. His muscles were even more pronounced than they'd been when we were kids, and for a brief moment I wish my body had been the same. But as his hands grasped at my hips, tugging me closer, I stopped caring.

No time had passed. Years had passed. Dreams and memories and many, many, self-pleasure moments. But nothing I'd imagined came close to the feeling of this man pressed against me. All too soon, he pulled away, and I whimpered like a dog who'd been deprived its pets. I wanted more pets, damn it.

"So eager, like always," he chuckled, his voice a deep rumble in his throat. "But hush, now, your time is about to come."

I had no idea what he meant. And I didn't care, other than the fact that something was about to happen to me... and if it was with him, that was perfectly fine with me. My eyes couldn't pull away from him, taking in every sinew of his body I knew so well. His ass was as tight as it had ever been, his cock hard and proud, something that had been carved just as delicately as this entire building. I wanted to jump on him, sit on his cock and scream his name. I wanted to watch his eyes as I rode him, regardless of those around us, seeing the brightest, blinding blue eyes as he erupted with pleasure. Despite the black mask that covered the upper portion of his face, I could still see them as he gazed at the crowd around us.

Around me, the music quieted, the gyrating and movement from the bodies so lost to each other slowly untangling. Chests heaved with labored breathing, skin slick with sweat and other things, and eyes all turned to me.

No, to Christian.

"*La Petite Mort,*" he started, when the crowd had gathered around us. The urge to cross my arms to cover my naked breasts arose once more, but I resisted and gritted my teeth, steeling myself. "We come to give in to the desires with which rage inside of us all. We do with no judgement, no ill will, and perfect acceptance."

"No judgement. No ill will. Perfect acceptance," the crowd around us repeated in unison.

"But tonight, is a special night. For you see, we have a new one amongst us," he gestured toward me, his eyes lingering as they trailed a burning path along my body. I shivered under his gaze and looked out to the crowd, their eyes doing the same. "Haven."

"Your desires are safe here, Haven," the crowd said.

"I confess, I already know Haven's desires. You see, I knew her when we were young and in college, and her desires were the same then as they are now. You can see them through where she migrated to, from the wetness coloring her panties as she'd taken in all of you and your embraces.

"For she is one to be watched; her pleasure is to be shared - as she receives carnal pleasure, she also receives it from the hungry eyes of those around her."

"Exhibition!" The crowd roared loudly, excited, clearly pleased with the private kink of mine Christian had so boldly lay out for all the room to see. It would've irked me if one, he hadn't been right and two... well I wasn't sure what two would be.

The man who'd so long haunted my masturbation turned to me, his eyes expectant as he took me in once more. He glanced from me to the scarlet couch.

"Desire doesn't come to those who do not reach for it," he murmured, so softly I could barely catch the words.

"Desire doesn't come to those who do not reach for it!" The crowd echoed, surprising me that they could hear the words that had seemed so private. Their eyes were curious, watching my every move.

They wanted to know if I was going to reach out and take what was offered. They were willing participants; more, they were just as desperate for me to be touched as my body was. The wetness Christian had mentioned was true - I'd been turned on since I'd arrived inside the room. Hell, I'd been turned on since the moment the Golden Girls had removed my gown. I so desperately wanted to reach for that desire, to grab ahold of it and wrap it around my naked skin. I wanted the moment of sheer bliss of a rock-hard cock penetrated me and the entirety of those around me gathered to view it.

This was different than the last time I'd had a public experience, though. That had been small, unknown in regard to whether anyone saw or didn't see. It was small stuff, minor; not this. This was big, and, in all fairness, it was exactly what I wanted. Hunger permeated the air, heady in its thickness; this was exactly what they all wanted as well.

Before I could change my mind, I took a step toward the couch. And another. Approaching it further, I was surprised to find it wasn't merely a couch. It was much larger up close and personal - the size of at the minimum a twin sized bed. It curved like a chaise lounge, one side rising up similar to a headboard. I glimpsed hooks at the top and bottom, clearly spots to anchor cuffs for those whose pleasure steered toward that sort of thing.

Lowering myself on to it gingerly, hoping I didn't lose my footing, I was pleased to find it was soft but firm at the same time, the velvet a chilled caress against the skin that came in contact with it. As I perched on the edge, looking up at Christian, the crowd as a whole cheered, the man in question's face alighting in a blinding smile. I knew, even through his mask, that it would've changed his entire expression, the muscles in his jaw releasing tension he always held.

The music started up again, the same hypnotic rhythm that had played before, and I idly wondered if it was one song on repeat, or a bunch of songs that all sounded the same. My internal meanderings were cut short, however, when Christian dropped to his knees in front of me, his strong hands gripping my ankles and pulling my legs. I gasped as he spread me open, my wet, panty-clad center exposing to the air and the crowd. I looked up, only to see expectant eyes, hands moving against themselves, or others, as they took in our display.

"Christian," I groaned, unsure of what I wanted, but knowing it was something only he could give me.

"Just as beautiful as ever," he breathed, his lips trailing kisses from my ankle to my knee, gently biting the tender skin behind through my fishnet stockings. I'd never cursed not being completely naked in this place more than at that exact moment. While he was warm, his kisses wet through the fabric, I desperately wanted to feel him, skin on skin.

As if reading my mind, Christian gently tugged on my shoe, allowing it to drop to the marble floor beside him. He repeated the gesture on the other side, before his hands trailed up my leg to the soft skin of my thigh. I moaned as his fingers reached the lace there, toying with it against my sensitive skin before peeling it down. The second was gone just as quickly, the barely-there material lost amongst the crowd who'd moved closer, to get a better view.

It was an epiphany as I realized that while my kink was having others view my pleasure, for others their pleasure kink came from watching. And the eagerness of those people was intoxicating.

Moving quickly, Christian's fingers replaced the skin that was exposed, his hands trailing teasing lines up my legs, my thighs. His hand grazed center as he moved, and I moaned, missing his touch as it flitted away.

"Christian," I whined again, to which he chuckled, his head ducking between my legs to kiss first my inner thigh, and then through my panties. I was about to complain again, but his tongue trailed the soft fabric, further wetting them, and causing my head to fall back and my eyes to close. He repeated the gesture, his strong hands grasping my knees and holding them open, allowing him full access to the most sensitive part of my body. He licked me through my panties, nibbling gently, and I buried my fingers into his hair, gripping at him, forcing him to stop.

"More."

This time it was a demand he knew all too well. I wasn't the most patient of women, a trait he knew and always managed to put up with. Between the pre-show of this party, and his ministrations between my legs, I wanted to feel him. I wanted him to actually touch me, to bury his fingers into my and make me scream. I wanted so much more than a censored popsicle treatment. I gyrated my hips in suggestion, and his lips quirked up again.

Christian glanced around, a motion that confused me until two men appeared on each side of me. Before I could ask any questions, the each grabbed a side of my panties and ripped, the soft fabric falling away from me before they stepped back again. I peered at them, taking in their chiseled bodies and hungry eyes, before my gaze flitted back to the man in front of me.

"We all have our desires, Haven. They don't wish to join in - give them a little of the desire you expect from them."

Dropping his head once more, Christian buried his face in my core, his tongue trailing a heated path along my outer lips before a finger tentatively played with my opening. I no longer cared who may want to join in; if their kink was ripping my panties off, they could rip every pair I owned so long as it was followed by the tongue of the man between my legs.

A moan sounded around amongst the rhythmic music and it took me a moment to realize it hadn't come from me, even if it had echoed my mind. I briefly noted a woman sitting, not too far from the couch, a man's head buried between her legs as well, his motions matching that of the one before me. It was hot and erotic, and a moan escaped my lips once more as Christian found my clit and sucked.

"I want you, all of you Christian. Please."

I hated that I was begging. But it had been so, so long, since I'd felt this much intensity. Since I'd wanted to be fucked as badly as I did right in this moment. It had been so long since I'd wanted to be fucked because of passion and desire, rather than to scratch an itch that was a necessity.

Christian understood and stood, his cock still standing proud, and, now that it was eye level, I leaned forward, capturing him in my mouth. My pussy flooded as he groaned in pleasure, halting in his movements, his hips involuntarily arching forward, pushing deeper into my mouth. I swirled my tongue around the head, toying with him, before drawing away slightly. My hands reached around him, grasping his ass and pulling him deeper into my mouth. His hands grasped at my hair, holding my head in place as he gently thrust in and out between my lips. Glancing up I saw his eyes were closed, his head thrown back, a Greek God in the throes of pleasure. It was one of the hottest things I'd ever seen.

The men around us groaned in unison with Christian as I toyed with him, my fingers caressing his balls as well. I pulled away to take them in, some with their cocks in another woman's mouth, some holding their erections in their palms. It was a powerful feeling, giving them the pleasure I was giving Christian, their need and desire for me to continue giving and receiving pleasure seductive.

"Evil woman," Christian murmured above the bass beat, and I grinned up at him innocently.

"Me?" I fluttered my eyelashes at him, a gesture I wasn't sure could be seen through my mask, but not caring. I felt like a superhero and was enjoying every single moment of this.

Leaning down, Christian grasped my legs and pulled me completely onto the couch, spreading my legs and propping himself between them. He rubbed his cock on my folds, the head coating itself in my juices. I writhed beneath him, desperate, wanting him inside me. I could feel the gazes of those around us, their energy, and knew they wanted it just as badly as I did. I'd never been one for delayed gratification, and I wanted what I wanted, when I wanted it.

"Now," I demanded, arching my hips in a futile attempt to capture his cock. Instead, the motion ground him against my clit harder and I grit my teeth, refusing to allow sound to escape my lips. I repeated the motion, only for the same result, which wasn't unpleasant but got me no closer to my end goal.

"God damn it," I swore, ignoring the satisfied glint in Christian's eyes. I knew he was enjoying it, the desperation that swirled inside of me, just as I was, in some deep dark part of me. Impatient, I reached between us, gripping his cock firmly in my hands and placing the head of his erection at my center. I was already soaking wet, my body drenched with its desire for him, and I pushed myself onto him, a satisfied hiss leaving my lips as his cock finally filled me.

A chorus of the same hiss sounded around us, the reminder that we were being watched and providing pleasure to everyone around us. It was a heady feeling, to give in a way that cost me nothing. I glanced around to find several women bent over, their partners penetrating them the way Christian's cock was me; some were laying prone on the floor, mirroring our actions. It was erotic and taboo, and I squeezed my eyes closed as I felt my blood warming at the sight.

Christian remained still, his cock throbbing inside me, and I gyrated my hips against him, grinding on him, hoping he'd move. But he didn't. He allowed me to steal the pleasure I so longed for, on my own terms, the thought of which felt just as good as if he was taking the lead. And so I remained where I was, frustrated and placated, at the same time, his cock just inside my pussy, but not far enough for me to get the entirety of what I wanted.

After what felt like forever, Christian rocked back on his heels, the tip of his cock slipping out and I whined in protest, only for him to thrust back into me, hard, stealing my breath and any sound I may have been capable of making. His cock hit the end of me, brushing almost painfully against my cervix, and he repeated the motion, this time a moan escaping my lips.

Strong hands grasped at my breasts, Christian's fingers gripping them for stability, his thumbs toying with my nipples in between his punishing thrusts. Leaning down, his lips caught mine, his tongue entwining with mine for just a moment before he withdrew and pulled away from me.

This time it was Christian who made the first move, pulling my hand and helping me to sit up and then to my knees. He moved around behind me, his body molding to my ass and my back, his hands spreading my legs to cradle his width.

"Desire doesn't come to those who do not reach for it" he murmured in my ear, his head turning to take in the crowd around us. I followed his gaze, wetness pooling between my legs as I noted others around us had frozen, their eyes alight as they watched Christian position the head of his cock to my pussy. He hesitated, only for a second, prolonging the moment for everyone, me included. And then, he thrust deep into me, a growl escaping his chest as he seated himself inside me, my toes curling.

The intensity of the music around us had sped up, and Christian matched its tempo, one that left me breathless as each thrust brought me closer and closer to the edge. It was delicious. It was hard and fast, and his cock knew the exact places inside me that felt the best. The slight down curve in his erection created a never-ending G-spot connection, and I groaned and moaned as he pumped into me. His hands gripped my ass at my hips, pulling me into him, faster and faster.

"Oh shit, I'm going to cum."

My words did nothing to slow him, his rhythm staying the same, and I came around him, vaguely hearing others doing the same. I skyrocketed, my soul leaving my body, the absolute satisfaction coursing through my blood enough to be the same high as drugs. I floated, only to be slammed back into my body by the sharp smack of Christian's hand landing on my ass.

"Stay with me. You're going to cum again, and this time it will be with me," Christian growled, his balls slapping against my folds as he thrust harder and deeper than I thought possible. It was like he was a machine, with nothing that could stop the piston-like pumping of his hips into me as his cock thrust within me. With each motion I could feel my thighs quivering, my breath catching. His motions were almost painful, though delicious in the friction he was creating between my legs.

Christian's breaths were coming quicker, groans of male pleasure escaping him and from the crowd gathered around us. I shot a glance over to see another man fucking a woman from behind and it was enough, my body tightening around Christian's cock, just as he screamed out his release. Profanity poured from his mouth, his thrusts jerking as he came, slowing his pace. His chest molded to my back as we tried to breathe, our bodies struggling in unison to find oxygen. It was as if all the air had been pulled from the room. My pussy was sore, and I knew I'd be walking funny tomorrow, but this had been more than worth it. More than any dream I'd ever dreamed and worth every second I'd searched for *La Petit Mort*.

I woke up in my plush, queen-sized bed, my pillows a barrier between me and the rest of the world. My white down comforter was pulled up and the room fans were on. I still wore my black gown I'd removed the previous evening, but my stockings and my panties were still mysteriously missing.

Getting home the night before was a blur.

Christian and I'd spent a few moments recovering from our ministrations and, with an eruptive round of applause from the crowd, he'd taken me to a side room where we could shower. I was lucky he'd already cum because after having been celibate for entirely too long, there was just no way I could go again. Not that I didn't want to - I did. I wanted to go again, and again, and again… it was like riding a bike - you always remembered how but got to go longer with practice. I wanted a night of hours like we'd just had, the crowd included.

But, in those moments, Christian had gently washed my body, murmuring words I could barely hear. I felt drunk, though I knew I wasn't. I was completely, one hundred percent sated, my brain in outer space and words were foreign to me. After he'd washed me, he'd mentioned seeing me soon, and the Golden Girls had re-dressed me and Lawrence had been waiting for me to take me home.

I must've fallen asleep on the short drive, because I'd opened my eyes when Lawrence had gingerly picked me up and carried me to the elevator and to my house. He'd had me put in my code and placed me softly on my bed before tipping his hand, whispering words of farewell, and leaving. After that, it felt like entirely too much effort to move, and I'd simply stayed where he'd left me... mostly.

As I'd imagined, my pussy was sore, but in the most delicious sense of the word. It was sore in the having been treated exactly the way I wanted it to be, way. With every step I took toward the kitchen, I relived the previous evening, and the experience I'd had.

La Petite Mort was real. And it was more than I could've ever hoped for.

Pouring a glass of water, I froze as my doorbell rang. I wasn't expecting anyone, and I was off work, so it wasn't a coworker. Maybe it was Christian? I didn't remember telling him where I lived, but as I was pretty certain he was the one who'd extended the invitation to me, it would've made sense he knew where to find me. He clearly knew where I worked. And how to get me off.

I made my way to the door, peering through the peephole, but finding no one standing there. I opened

Exhibition

The End of *Exhibition*.

Read more from Juli Valenti by visiting her website at www.julivalenti.com.

JULI VALENTI

About Juli

Juli Valenti is a contemporary romance author who just can't seem to make up her mind. She enjoys writing everything from sweet and funny romantic comedies, to ugly cry, heartbreaking stories, and even romantic suspense.

Her newest series, Redemption Reigns MC, has become a pivotal turning point in motorcycle club romance novels, changing the pace and bring diversity to a world run by men... which is so much fun!

Juli is from Bentonville, Arkansas, home of Wal-Mart and currently resides in Florida with her two sons just minutes from the beach.

Juli is currently working to bring more MC novels to the table, as well as more collaborations with Author Rene Folsom, and a bunch more! Keep on the look out and remember to sign up for her newsletter to stay up to date.

Follow Juli

Receive New Release Updates

www.julivalenti.com/newsletter/

Website

www.julivalenti.com

Facebook

www.facebook.com/authorjulivalenti

Twitter

@thejulivalenti

Amazon

www.amazon.com/author/julivalenti

JULI VALENTI

Juli's Books

The Redemption Reigns MC Series
Poet (Redemption Reigns MC Book 1)
Artist (Redemption Reigns MC Book 2)
Fallen (Redemption Reigns MC Book 3)
Mercy (Redemption Reigns MC Book 4)

The Distracted Series
Greatest Distraction (Distracted Book 1)
Global Distraction (Distracted Book 2)
All Roads Lead to Jackson (Distracted Book 2.5)

The Chance Series
Pieces in Chance (Chance Book 1)
Coming Soon – Another Chance (Chance Book 2)

The Addiction Series
Sadie Hawkins (Addiction Book 1)
Coming Soon – Morning Glory (Addiction Book 2)

Favorite Things Series
(co-authored with Rene Folsom)
Adventurous, Bound, & Charming

Taunt: A Twisted Wolf Tale
A Little Broken
Vancleave (Learning to Submit Book 1)
All Our Love (Anthology)

Made in United States
Orlando, FL
13 September 2023